The Adventures of Commander Zack Proton and the Wrong Planet

By Brian Anderson
Illustrated by Doug Holgate

Aladdin Paperbacks

New York • London • Toronto • Sydney

To Samantha, for launching Zack Proton into the
universe, and to Molly, for helping him fly straight.
May your stars shine ever brighter. —B. A.

For Allyson. —D. H.

ALADDIN PAPERBACKS
An imprint of Simon & Schuster Children's Publishing Division
1230 Avenue of the Americas, New York, NY 10020
Text copyright © 2007 by Brian Anderson
Illustrations copyright © 2007 by Doug Holgate
All rights reserved, including the right of
reproduction in whole or in part in any form.
ALADDIN PAPERBACKS and related logo are
registered trademarks of Simon & Schuster, Inc.
Designed by Sammy Yuen
The text of this book was set in Zolano Serif BTN.
Manufactured in the United States of America
First Aladdin Paperbacks edition April 2007
6 8 10 9 7 5
Library of Congress Control Number 2006940768
ISBN-13: 978-1-4169-1366-5
0816 QVE

CONTENTS

CONTENTS

CHAPTER ONE

This Little Piggie Went to Bounceback

I will not scream," Omega Chimp promised himself in the cockpit of his spaceship, the *Giant Slayer*. "I will not scream."

Pa-TIK
pa-TOK
Pa-TIK
Pa-TIK
pa-TOK
Pa-TIK
Pa-TIK
pa-TOK
pa-TOK
Pa-TIK
Pa-TIK

"I will not scream, I will not scream, I will not scream."

"Stop it! Stop it, already!" Omega Chimp screamed toward the back of the ship. "You're driving me crazy!"

Thirty-seven hours and two seconds later . . .

"He can't stop," Commander Zack Proton replied. "He'll lose." Zack's eyes followed the ball back and forth across the table. "That's it, Effie, keep going. You can beat him!"

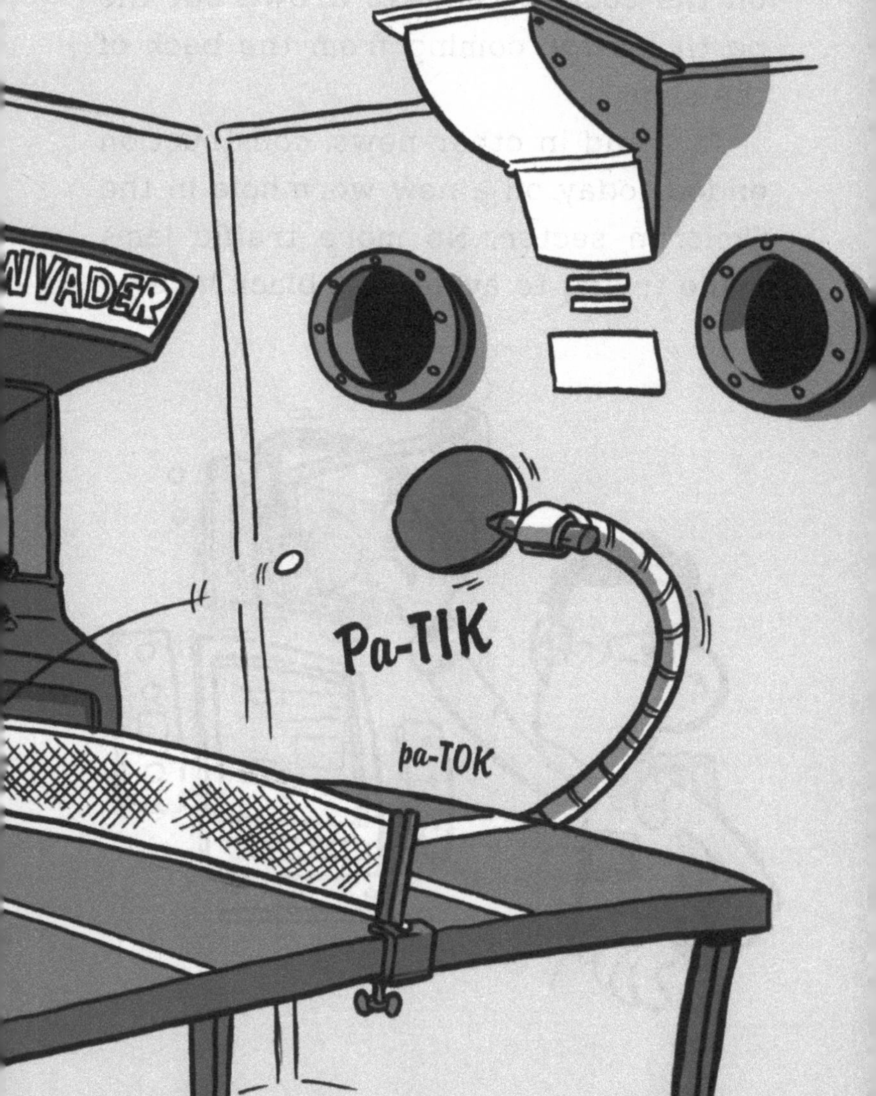
NVADER
Pa-TIK
pa-TOK

Omega Chimp turned up the volume on the cockpit radio to drown out the *pa-tik pa-tok* coming from the back of the ship.

". . . and in other news, construction ended today on a new wormhole in the Omicron sector. No more traffic jams while trying to avoid that black hole."

"What's a wormhole?" Zack asked.

Omega Chimp practically jumped out of his skin. "Don't sneak up on me like that," he said. Omega Chimp reached for a banana to calm his nerves.

What's a Wormhole?

A wormhole is:

1. The part of the apple that is
   pre-eaten for you.
2. A hole in the ground that is too small for you
   to fall into (unless you are very, very small!).
π.* A tunnel through space
   that works like a shortcut to a
   location that is trillions of miles away.
4. All of these except the third one.
5. All of these, including the third one.
6. None of these except the third one.
7. Only the third one.
8. What was the question?

*close enough

The news continued. "Planet Bounceback is now the proud owner of sixteen million pigs, delivered today from planet Pigfarm, more than half a universe away."

"Leapin' leptons!" Zack cried. "The *Risky Rascal* was carrying sixteen million pigs! We've got to get to Bounceback right away!"

Omega Chimp pulled a map out from his dashboard console. "According to this star chart, Bounceback is only two stars away in the Gamma Triton system. We should be there in less than an hour."

WAIT A PARSEC! WHO ARE THESE GUYS?

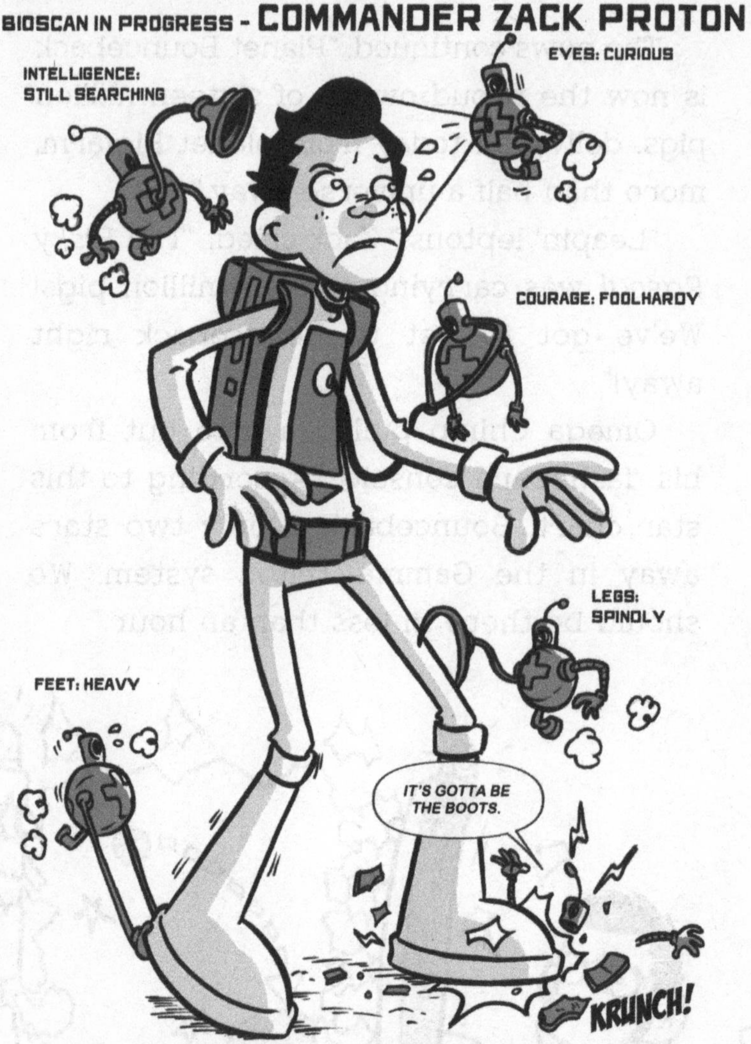
BIOSCAN IN PROGRESS - COMMANDER ZACK PROTON
INTELLIGENCE: STILL SEARCHING
EYES: CURIOUS
COURAGE: FOOLHARDY
LEGS: SPINDLY
FEET: HEAVY
IT'S GOTTA BE THE BOOTS.
KRUNCH!

SUBJECT FELL OUT THE BACK DOOR OF HIS SPACESHIP, THE *RISKY RASCAL*, AND HAS BEEN LOOKING FOR IT EVER SINCE.

MEDICAL REPORT IN PROGRESS –
OMEGA CHIMP

INTELLIGENCE: HIGH

PATIENCE: LOW

EYES: ANGRY

FINGERS: TEN

DIET: BANANAS

TOES: FINGERS

SUBJECT PICKED UP COMMANDER ZACK PROTON FROM SPACE, AND HAS BEEN REGRETTING IT EVER SINCE.

FE-203
DIAGNOSTIC CHECKUP

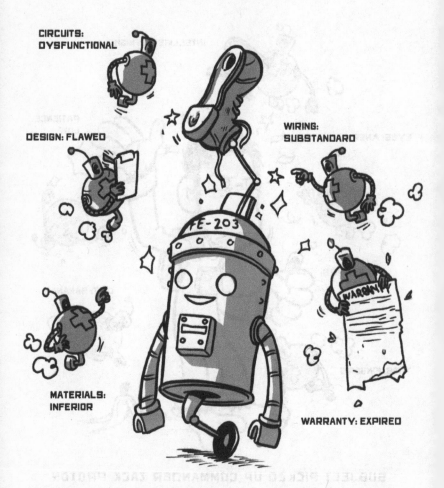

CIRCUITS:
DYSFUNCTIONAL

DESIGN: FLAWED

WIRING:
SUBSTANDARD

MATERIALS:
INFERIOR

WARRANTY: EXPIRED

THIS FE-203 PERSONAL DROID IS SO DEFECTIVE THAT IT WOULD REQUIRE EXPENSIVE UPGRADES BEFORE IT CAN BE SOLD FOR SCRAP.

CHAPTER TWO

Now You See It . . .

Less than an hour of *pa-tik pa-tok* later, they approached orbit around Bounceback.

"We're here!" Omega Chimp called out toward the back of the ship. Zack and Effie arrived in the cockpit a moment later.

"Two to nothing," Effie said proudly. "I'm winning."

"Aren't you also losing?" Omega Chimp asked.

"Of course not," Zack answered. "There's only one Effie, so how can he be winning *and* losing? If he's here, he can't be there, and if he's there, he can't be here, and here he is, so there you go."

2-0

Omega Chimp just shook his head. "Get ready to beam down," he said, handing them their wristbands.

"But isn't there supposed to be a planet?" Effie asked nervously, looking out the window of the ship.

"It's right . . ." Omega Chimp scanned the controls. They were orbiting empty space. The planet was gone. "That's impossible," he said. "It was there a minute ago. I saw it myself. The computer saw it too."

"Leapin' leptons, now our computer has lost its mind too!" Zack said.

"I have not lost my mind," Omega Chimp replied as he tapped at the keyboard of his ship's computer. A new map of the universe appeared on Omega Chimp's screen. "This star chart says Bounceback is ten galaxies away from here!"

"Ten galaxies away!" Zack replied. "How could that have happened?"

"Why don't we beam down and ask someone on the planet below?" Effie suggested, pointing out the window.

Zack and Omega Chimp looked out the window. They were suddenly in orbit around a small, green planet.

"What's that planet doing there?" Zack asked.

"There's only one way to find out," Omega Chimp replied. He grabbed a banana and pressed the transporter button three times. Omega Chimp, Zack Proton, and FE-203 instantaneously disappeared in a shimmer of rainbow light.

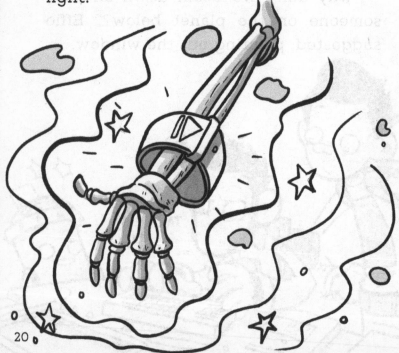

CHAPTER THREE

New Pork City

Zack, Omega Chimp, and FE-203 reappeared on the planet below with a twinkling of light. They were surrounded by thousands and thousands of pigs.

"Leapin' leptons!" Zack cried, looking around. "What a humongous herd of hogs, what a sizeable swarm of swine—"

"What a seriously sickening stench!" said Omega Chimp. "Pee-yoo! What could any planet possibly want with this many pigs?"

Just then the pigs saw Omega Chimp's banana and started jumping up to get a bite for themselves.

"Get down," he scolded them. Omega Chimp held his banana high above his head, but the pigs only jumped higher. "Make them stop jumping," he said to Zack.

"How?" Zack asked.

"I don't care how, just—Hey, stop that!" he cried.

The swarm of pigs hopped all around Omega Chimp like pesky pink popcorn. Omega Chimp stretched and dodged and stood on tippy toes, trying to keep his banana away from them, but the pigs finally knocked him off balance, and down he went. Omega Chimp and his tasty, sweet banana disappeared under a horde of hungry pigs.

A loud *sluuuurrrp* came from the bottom of the pig pile, and then the pigs wandered off licking their lips. Omega Chimp stood up. His spacesuit was dirty and torn, his banana was gone, and he smelled like a dozen filthy pigs all rolled into one.

"Are you through playing with the piggies?" Zack asked impatiently. "We need to find the *Risky Rascal*."

"Why don't we ask him?" said Effie. In the distance an alien tailor was wrapping a tape measure around a pig's belly.

They waded through the sea of pigs toward the alien. He stretched his measuring tape around one pig's belly after another, and wrote down all the numbers. The pigs squealed nervously as he grabbed each of them.

"Good and plump!" the alien said, releasing one pig. "Nice and round!" he said, after measuring the belly of another. He looked at his latest measurement and shook his head. "Still too small," he said. "You're not eating enough. Fatten up already! Your first performance is in two weeks."

"What performance?" Zack asked.

The alien glanced up, startled. "The audience is already arriving!" he cried. "Our million-pig opera is a success!"

"Million-pig opera?" Omega Chimp asked.

"We're starting small, with only a million singing pigs," the tailor answered. "But eventually we hope to include every pig on the planet. It'll be the largest pig opera in the universe!" He patted a pig on the head. The pig didn't look happy.

"A million singing pigs!" Zack said. "I can't wait to hear that!"

"I can," Omega Chimp muttered.

"Oink," one of the pigs added.

"We've already made some wonderful outfits for the pigs to wear in the show," the tailor said, "but the pigs are too small. They don't fit the costumes! There's not enough time to make the clothes smaller, so we have to make the pigs bigger."

"We're looking for the *Risky Rascal*," Omega Chimp said. "It's the spaceship that brought all these pigs to Bounceback."

"That ship landed ten galaxies away from here," the tailor replied.

"Wrong planet!" Zack cried, glaring at Omega Chimp. "We're supposed to be daring space heroes, not wrong-turn tourists."

"But my star charts—," Omega Chimp began.

"Those star charts are wrong half the time," the alien answered, getting to his feet. "It was nice meeting you, but I have many more pigs to measure. See you at the show!" The tailor scurried off, trailing his tape measure behind. The pigs gazed up sadly at Zack, Effie, and Omega Chimp.

"I don't think these pigs want to be opera singers," Effie said.

"Why would they?" Omega Chimp asked. "Nobody in his right mind is going to pay money to listen to a million pigs trying to sing."

"I hope we can get front-row seats!" Zack replied.

CHAPTER FOUR

UV or Not UV

Zack, Effie, and Omega Chimp transported back to their ship. It would be a long trip to Bounceback, so Omega Chimp set the ship's controls on autopilot. Then he wrinkled his nose at the horrible pig smell coming from his spacesuit.

SNIFF
SNIFF

"Look at my spacesuit," Omega Chimp said. "It's filthy and it smells like pigs, but I can't wash it. It's the only suit I have, and I'm afraid it'll shrink."

Zack's eyes lit up. "I saw an ultra-violet dry-cleaning machine in a space-port once," he said. "I'm sure Effie can build one if you have all the parts."

"Not so fast," said Omega Chimp. "I remember what happened when he fixed my banana generator. It nearly killed us all."

"He won't touch your banana generator, will you, Effie?" Zack asked.

"Promise," Effie answered.

"I'm not going to regret this, am I?" asked Omega Chimp.

"Not for an instant," said Zack.

"I know it'll never work," Omega Chimp said with a sigh, "but at least it'll keep him from playing Ping-Pong all night."

Effie lit up all over. "I'll get started right away!" he said, and rolled off, beeping and clicking to himself.

"And don't use anything from the ship that has a yellow safety tag on it!" Omega Chimp called after him.

"I won't," Effie called back.

"It's nearly bedtime anyway," Zack said, "so why don't we just go to sleep, and by morning Effie should be just about finished."

Omega Chimp took a bath, then went to his sleeping cabin and put on his pajamas. He enjoyed a late-night banana snack, and before long Omega Chimp fell asleep to the sounds of Effie's tinkering.

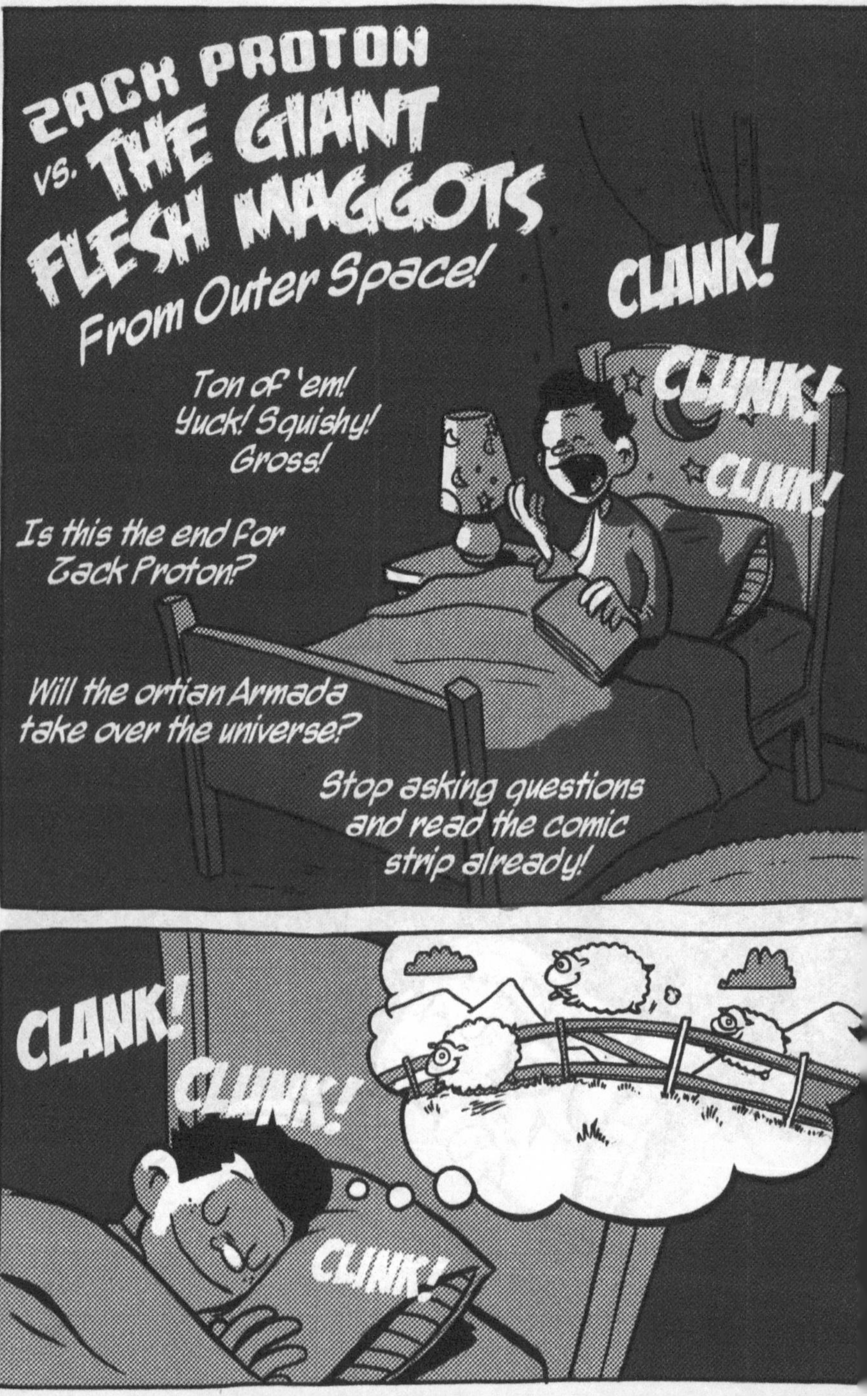
ZACK PROTON vs. THE GIANT FLESH MAGGOTS From Outer Space!
CLANK!
CLUNK!
CLINK!
Ton of 'em! Yuck! Squishy! Gross!
Is this the end for Zack Proton?
Will the ortian Armada take over the universe?
Stop asking questions and read the comic strip already!
CLANK!
CLUNK!
CLINK!

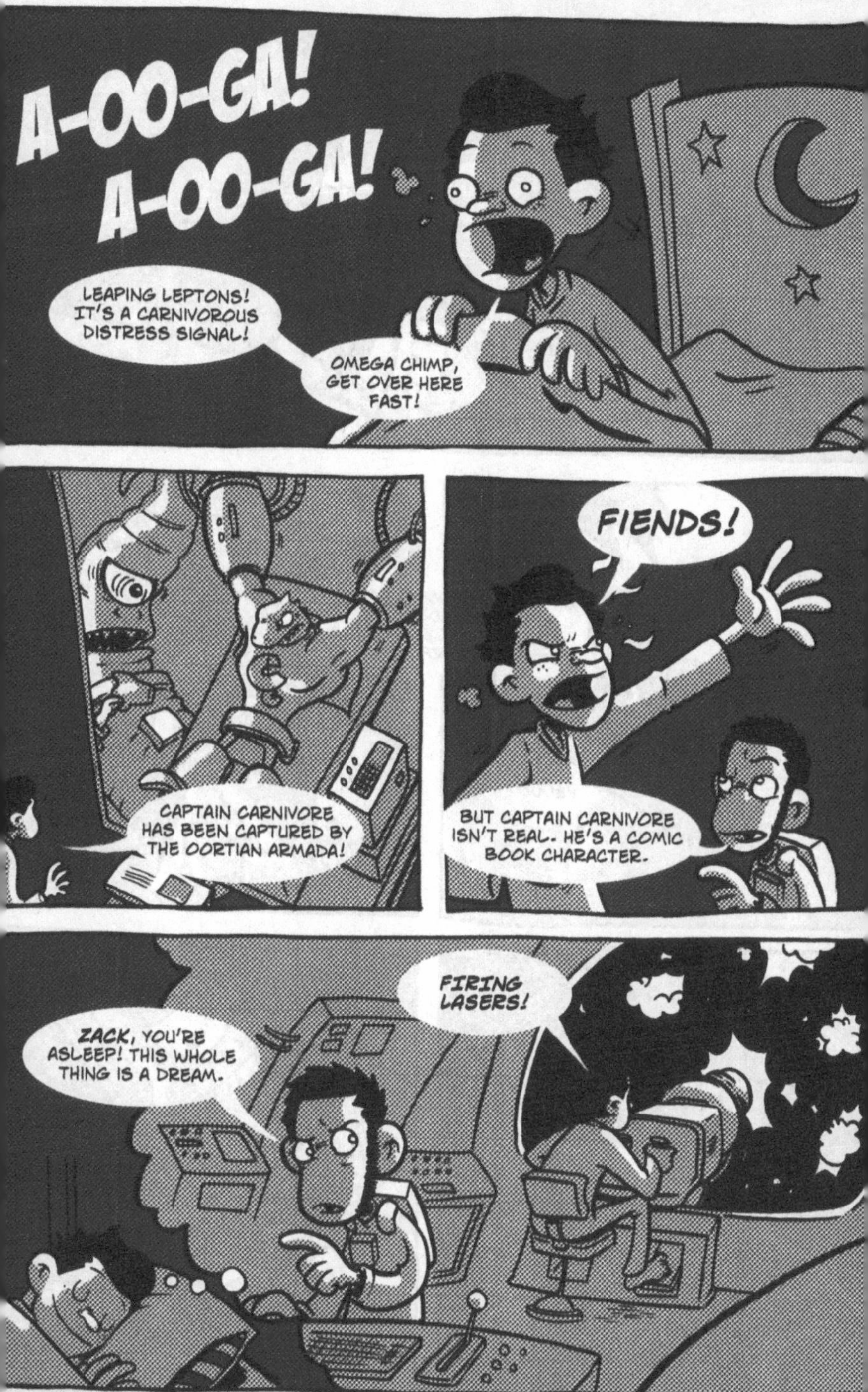
A-OO-GA!
A-OO-GA!
LEAPING LEPTONS! IT'S A CARNIVOROUS DISTRESS SIGNAL!
OMEGA CHIMP, GET OVER HERE FAST!
CAPTAIN CARNIVORE HAS BEEN CAPTURED BY THE OORTIAN ARMADA!
FIENDS!
BUT CAPTAIN CARNIVORE ISN'T REAL. HE'S A COMIC BOOK CHARACTER.
FIRING LASERS!
ZACK, YOU'RE ASLEEP! THIS WHOLE THING IS A DREAM.

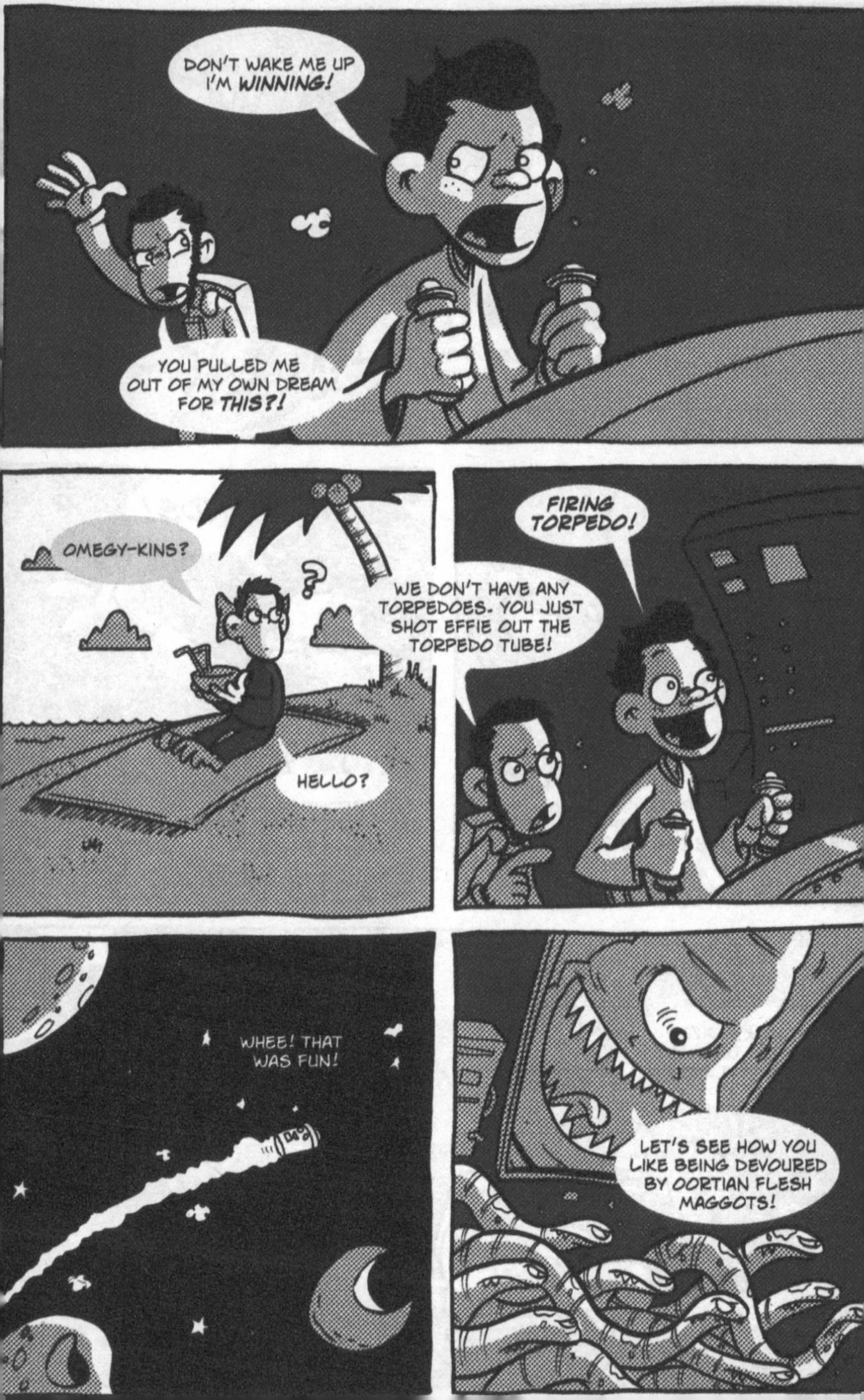
DON'T WAKE ME UP I'M WINNING!
YOU PULLED ME OUT OF MY OWN DREAM FOR THIS?!
OMEGY-KINS?
HELLO?
FIRING TORPEDO!
WE DON'T HAVE ANY TORPEDOES. YOU JUST SHOT EFFIE OUT THE TORPEDO TUBE!
WHEE! THAT WAS FUN!
LET'S SEE HOW YOU LIKE BEING DEVOURED BY OORTIAN FLESH MAGGOTS!

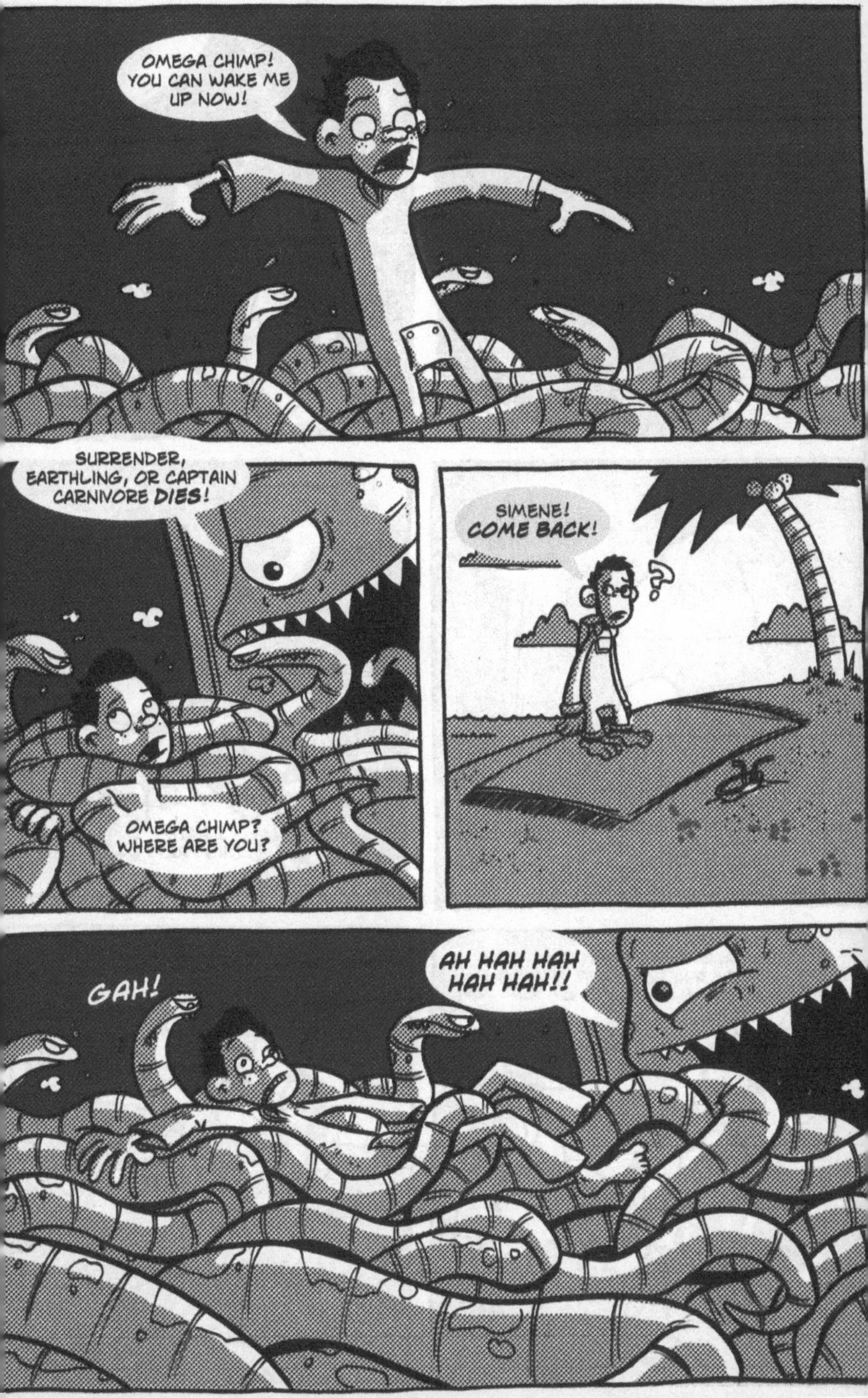
OMEGA CHIMP! YOU CAN WAKE ME UP NOW!
SURRENDER, EARTHLING, OR CAPTAIN CARNIVORE DIES!
OMEGA CHIMP? WHERE ARE YOU?
SIMENE! COME BACK!
GAH!
AH HAH HAH HAH HAH!!

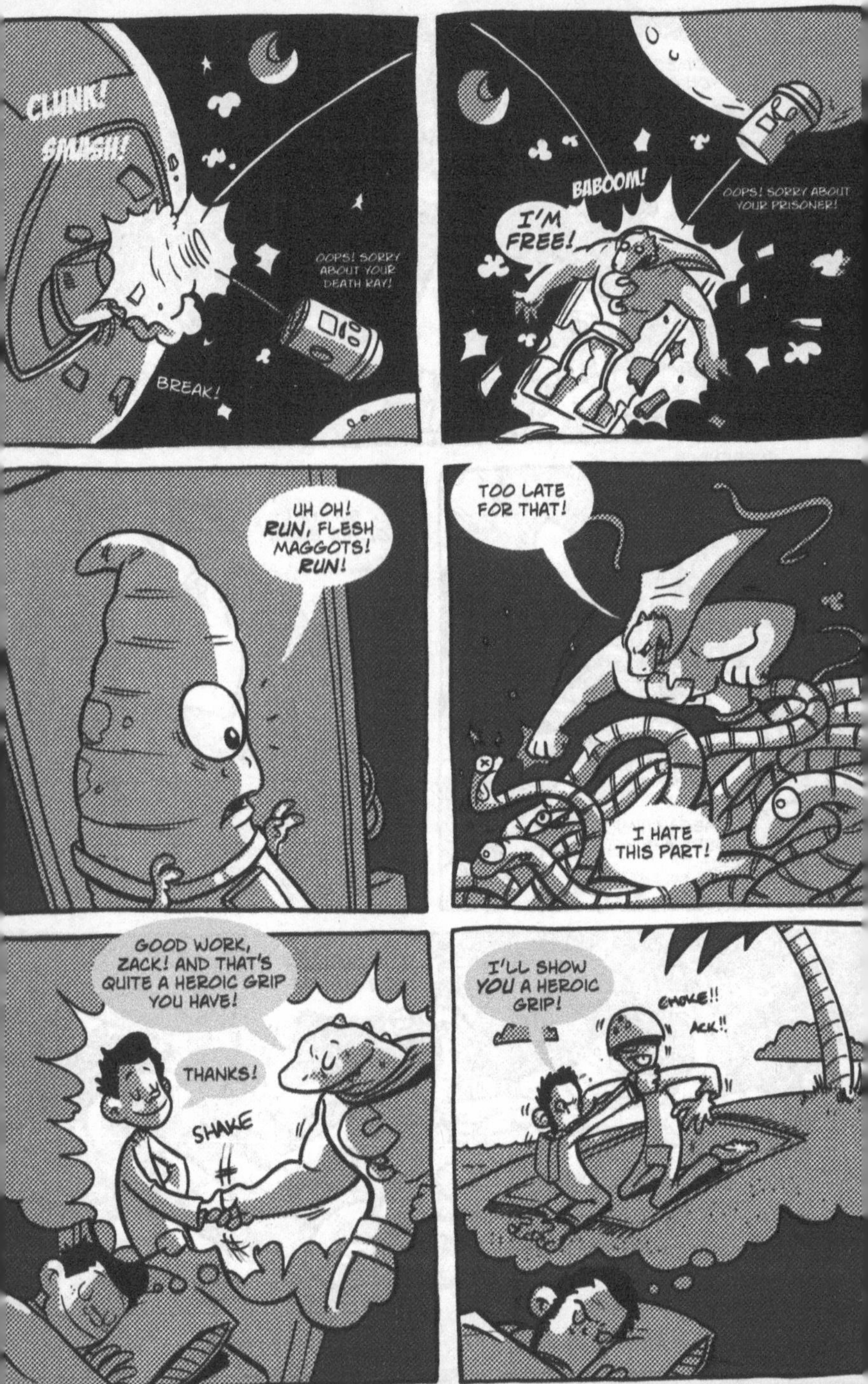
CLUNK!
SMASH!
OOPS! SORRY ABOUT YOUR DEATH RAY!
BREAK!
BABOOM!
I'M FREE!
OOPS! SORRY ABOUT YOUR PRISONER!
UH OH! RUN, FLESH MAGGOTS! RUN!
TOO LATE FOR THAT!
I HATE THIS PART!
GOOD WORK, ZACK! AND THAT'S QUITE A HEROIC GRIP YOU HAVE!
THANKS!
SHAKE
I'LL SHOW YOU A HEROIC GRIP!
CHOKE!!
ACK!!

CHAPTER FIVE

Taken to the Cleaners

When Omega Chimp awoke, the ship was quiet.

"All finished!" Effie called out.

Omega Chimp emerged from his room, wearing his pajamas.

"If you're going to dress like that from now on, maybe you should change your name to Pajama Chimp," said Zack.

"I'm only wearing these until my spacesuit is ready."

"Here's the machine. Isn't she a beauty?" said Effie proudly. "Just set your dirty spacesuit under this light and turn it on. Your suit will smell daisy fresh in no time."

Omega Chimp carefully laid out his silver spacesuit beneath the lightbulb. Effie turned the knob from off to low, and a bright purple light shined onto the spacesuit. The machine hummed quietly.

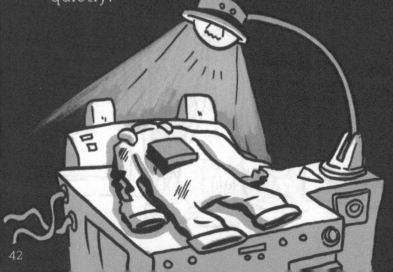

"I wasn't sure how much power it would take, so I made three different settings," Effie explained. "I made sure this machine would have enough power to clean anything. But you better not reach in with your hands when it's turned up all the way. That might not be safe."

"Let's just leave it on low," Omega Chimp said. The machine continued humming quietly, the ultraviolet light glowing brightly.

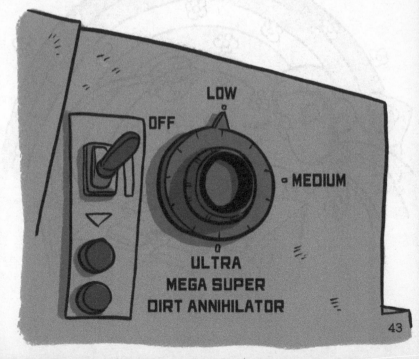

LOW

OFF

◦ MEDIUM

ULTRA
MEGA SUPER
DIRT ANNIHILATOR

"Your spacesuit looks all purple under that light," Zack said.

Omega Chimp sniffed the air. "I think it's working. My suit doesn't smell so bad anymore."

A minute later all the stains were gone, and there wasn't the slightest trace of pig smell. Omega Chimp's spacesuit smelled daisy fresh.

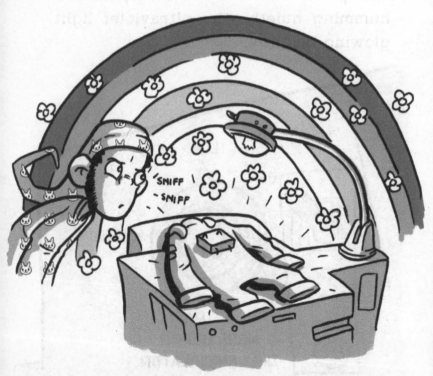

"It worked, Effie! That's amazing! You really are a robotic genius," said Omega Chimp.

Effie's lights flashed happily. He reached out to turn the knob to off. "Oops!" he said as he turned the knob in the wrong direction. "I think I broke it." The machine started shaking and rattling, and the lightbulb lit up the ship like an angry purple sun.

"Turn it off!" Omega Chimp yelled.

"I can't!" Effie answered, holding up the knob.

"My spacesuit," Omega Chimp screamed. "It's shrinking!" Omega Chimp reached to pull his spacesuit out of the raging machine.

"Not with your hands!" Effie warned him.

"I'm using my foot," Omega Chimp answered.

"Not with your feet, either," Effie added.

"This machine is going crazy!" Zack shouted over the loud buzzing. "What should we do?"

"Quick, grab all the dirty laundry you can find," said Effie.

Omega Chimp pulled the plug instead, and the machine sputtered and grumbled to a stop. Omega Chimp's spacesuit had shrunk to almost nothing and was still purple.

"What have you done!" he cried.

"Well, except for your spacesuit being only one inch tall and purple, I'd say Effie did a great job, wouldn't you?" Zack asked.

"I have nothing to wear!"

A computer voice interrupted them. "Approaching planetary orbit."

"I can't go down there in my pajamas!" Omega Chimp declared.

"You should have thought of that before you shrunk your spacesuit," Zack said, and tapped the transporter button three times. Seconds later, Zack, Effie, and Omega Chimp disappeared in a swirl of light.

CHAPTER SIX

You Can Lead a Pig to Opera, but You Can't Make Him Sing

Zack, Effie, and Omega Chimp reappeared on the planet in a twinkling flash. They found themselves once again surrounded by pigs, pigs, and more pigs.

"Why can't I just wait on my ship?" asked Omega Chimp.

"A genuine intergalactic space hero shows no fear, no weakness," said Zack. "Be brave, be bold, and pace proudly in your pajamas past the pigs."

"I look like a fool," said Omega Chimp.

"Sometimes it can be very hard to tell the difference between a genuine intergalactic space hero and a fool," said Zack.

"I have that problem a lot," Effie chimed in.

"You know," said Omega Chimp, looking around, "this planet looks just like the last one. The people, the buildings . . . even the pigs look the same."

"Your clothes are different," said Effie.

"We're ten galaxies away from that other planet," Zack said. "This time we're on Bounceback for sure. But just to be certain, let's ask somebody."

Nearby they saw an alien music teacher waving a conductor's baton. The pigs in front of her were dressed like kings, queens, princes, and princesses.

"Tra la la, fa la la," the teacher sang.

"Oink," the pigs replied.

"Let's try something else," she said. "Do re mi fa so la ti do!" she sang.

"Oink," the pigs replied.

"Oh dear," the music teacher said. "Only two weeks of rehearsal left and not one of you can sing a note!"

Zack, Effie, and Omega Chimp squeezed past some pigs, toward the music teacher. A pig dressed like a princess looked up at them with sad eyes, as though pleading for help.

"She doesn't look like a very happy princess," Zack said to the teacher.

"Oh, that's not a she," the music teacher replied, "That's a boy pig."

"Dressed like a princess?" Zack asked.

"No wonder he's not happy," Omega Chimp said.

"But you can't wear that costume to the opera," the alien music teacher said to Omega Chimp. "People might think you're part of the show."

"I do not look like a singing pig!" Omega Chimp protested.

"Are you making a pig opera too?" Zack asked the teacher. "We just came from another planet that has a million-pig opera."

"I knew it!" the music teacher said. "Once word got out about our marvelous pig opera, everybody would have one! Which planet was it? It was Bandwagon, wasn't it? Or those copycats on Metoo?"

"We never learned the name of the planet," Omega Chimp said. "It's ten galaxies away from here."

"Oh, that was Bounceback," the teacher replied.

"What! We're on the wrong planet *again*?" cried Zack.

CHAPTER SEVEN

A Senseless Census

Zack, Effie, and Omega Chimp were stumped. There were two identical planets full of pigs. One of them had to be Bounceback, but which one?

"We can't go by what the star charts say," said Omega Chimp. "And the people of each planet say the other one is Bounceback. How are we ever going to tell which one it is?"

Zack snapped his fingers. "I've got it," he said. "We count the pigs. The *Risky Rascal* was carrying sixteen million pigs, so if this planet has exactly sixteen million pigs, we'll know they must have come from my ship."

"It'll take years to count that many pigs!" said Omega Chimp. "And by the time we're done, their babies' babies will have babies."

"Then we just won't count the babies," Zack replied. "One, two, three . . ."

Omega Chimp turned to FE-203. "Effie, help me talk some sense into him, will you?"

"Sh!" replied Effie, "Twelve, thirteen, fourteen . . ."

Two hours later Omega Chimp was still shaking his head, and Zack and Effie were still counting pigs.

Zack pointed to each pig as he counted. "Eight thousand six hundred and fourteen . . . four thousand six hundred and eighteen . . . eight thousand six hundred and nineteen . . ."

"I already counted that one," said Effie.

"Which one?" Zack asked.

"That big, smelly one," Effie answered.

"They're all big and smelly," Zack answered. "Are you sure you counted him?"

"I counted him twice just to be certain," Effie replied.

"Effie, you can't count the pigs twice," Zack said.

"You want me to count them three times?"

Omega Chimp threw his arms into the air. "This is hopeless!" he cried.

60

CHAPTER EIGHT

Pig Breath

Leapin' leptons!" Zack said. "I've got a better idea. The *Risky Rascal* picked up all those banana peels from space to feed the pigs, remember?"*

"But the banana peels are gone by now," Omega Chimp replied. "The pigs would have eaten them all."

*If you don't remember, it's time to reread *The Adventures of Commander Zack Proton and the Red Giant*!

"So if their breath smells like bananas, then these are our pigs!"

Omega Chimp made a face. "I'm not going to smell a pig's breath."

"But you like banana smell," said Zack.

"But what if these aren't our pigs? Doesn't Effie have some kind of odor detector?"

Effie started rolling backward.

"You're not afraid, are you?" Zack asked.

A yellow streak flashed across Effie's lights. "No, but I'm a genuine intergalactic space hero like you, and smelling a pig's breath sounds a little . . . foolish."

"It's not foolish, Effie. It's heroic," Zack explained.

"Sometimes it can be very hard to tell the difference," added Omega Chimp.

"Well, okay. If you guys say so." Effie rolled up to the nearest pig and opened a panel on his side. A rubber nose on a rubber hose extended toward the pig. The curious pig leaned toward Effie's electronic nose. He looked at it curiously, and then snuffed right into it.

Effie's lights flickered in a spiraling pattern, and then he fell over and began rolling back and forth in the mud. Sickly green lights raced randomly across his surface. "Error, error, error . . ."

Paid Advertisment

Loony Lenny 'n' Larry's Discount Used Planets!

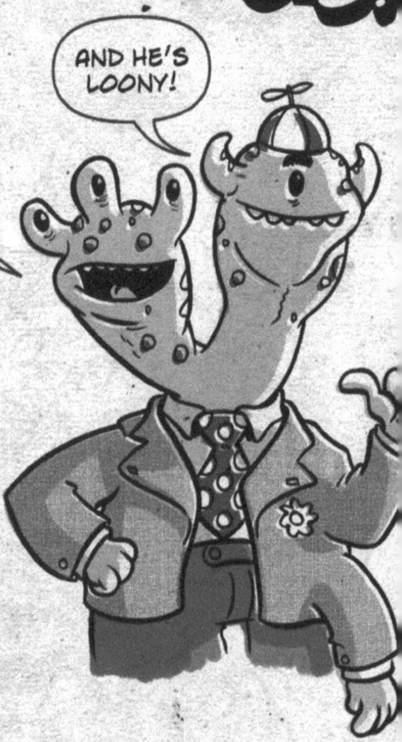
HE'S LENNY!
AND HE'S LOONY!
AND WE MUST BE CRAZY TO SELL PLANETS THIS CHEAP!

Check out these new listings!

Binary Star Vacation Home:
63 hours of sunshine in every 64-hour cycle. Tan until you burn in year long balmy 450 degree weather. Gorgeous sand beaches stretch for miles in every direction. Uncontaminated by water. Unpopulated.

Secluded Winter Hideaway -
Ice planet orbiting distant star. No neighbors, no traffic, no oxygen. Population: one gigantic hibernating subterranean ice troll. Previous owner died suddenly after waking troll. Must sell!

- COUPON -

Free moon with the purchase of ANY planet

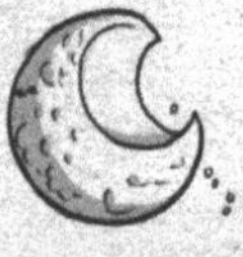

CHAPTER NINE

...Now You Don't

Zack pressed the transport button on Effie's wristband, and together the three of them beamed back up to their ship. Effie rolled back and forth on the floor of the spaceship, his lights blinking helplessly. "Error, error, error . . ."

REPAIRING YOUR FE-203 PERSONAL ROBOTIC ASSISTANT

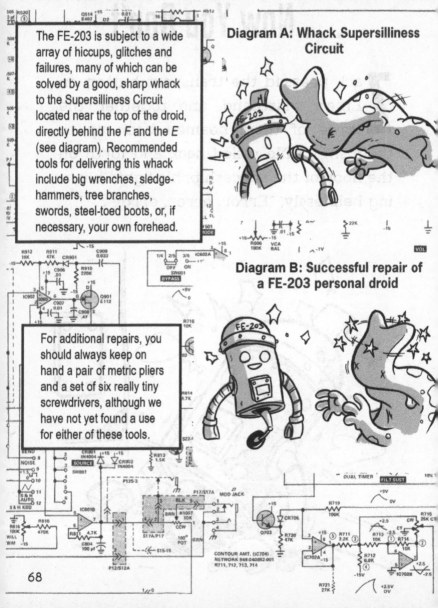

The FE-203 is subject to a wide array of hiccups, glitches and failures, many of which can be solved by a good, sharp whack to the Supersilliness Circuit located near the top of the droid, directly behind the *F* and the *E* (see diagram). Recommended tools for delivering this whack include big wrenches, sledge-hammers, tree branches, swords, steel-toed boots, or, if necessary, your own forehead.

Diagram A: Whack Supersilliness Circuit

Diagram B: Successful repair of a FE-203 personal droid

For additional repairs, you should always keep on hand a pair of metric pliers and a set of six really tiny screwdrivers, although we have not yet found a use for either of these tools.

Zack followed the repair instructions from the FE-203 manual, and Effie's lights started flashing in a pattern. "Thank you," he said.

"Well, Effie?" Zack asked. "Did the pig's breath smell like bananas?"

Effie's lights turned green as he remembered the smell. "I'm not sure," he said slowly. "I think a pig's breath smells the same no matter what you feed it."

"Then I guess it's back to counting," Zack said.

"Wait," said Omega Chimp. "Why didn't I think of this before? We can use the ship's sensors to count all the pigs at once."

Omega Chimp began flipping switches and turning dials on the control panel. "I'll program the computer for pigs only, and the scanner will ignore everything else on the planet. We'll know exactly how many pigs are on the planet in a matter of seconds."

Omega Chimp finished setting the controls and pressed a button. "There," he said, watching the display screen. "And the answer is . . ."

"Zero? Zero pigs? There must be something wrong," Omega Chimp said.

"No, I think that number is correct," said Effie, looking out the window. "It looks like all the pigs are gone."

"How can you tell that from all the way up here?" Omega Chimp asked.

"Because the whole planet is gone."

Zack and Omega Chimp rushed to the window. They were orbiting empty space.

CHAPTER TEN

Follow the Bouncing Ball

T hat's impossible!" Omega Chimp said. "Whole planets don't just vanish from space." Omega Chimp turned the ship's viewscopes in every direction. "There's nothing there, nothing at all. . . . Wait!"

A tiny speck of yellow appeared in the center of his video screen. At first it was just a yellow blob floating in space, then it began to look a little bit like an octopus, and finally they could see it clearly. . . .

"A banana peel!" they all shouted at the same time.

"The *Risky Rascal* was here!" said Zack.

"No wonder the people kept telling us the other planet was Bounceback," Omega Chimp said. He grabbed all of his old star charts and laid them side-by-side. "The location of Bounceback keeps changing on these charts. First it's here, and then it's ten galaxies away. Then it's right back here again, and then it's ten galaxies away. Do you realize what this means?"

"They get a lot of frequent-flyer miles?" Effie guessed.

"They have to forward their mail every day?" suggested Zack.

"It means *both* planets are Bounce-back!" Omega Chimp said. "It just keeps bouncing back and forth in space forever, like . . . like . . ."

"Like a giant Ping-Pong ball playing all by itself?" Effie asked.

"Yes!" Omega Chimp said. "Exactly like that."

"I wonder who's winning," Zack said.

CHAPTER ELEVEN

Bounceback Bounces Back. Or Not.

But how can a whole planet just hop back and forth in space like that?" asked Zack.

"There's only one explanation," Omega Chimp answered. "Bounceback must sit right on the edge of a wormhole, and the planet keeps falling through to the other side."

"Then all we have to do is wait here long enough and Bounceback will bounce back," Zack said.

An hour later there was no sign of the planet Bounceback. Two hours later there was *still* no sign of Bounceback.

"What if it never returns?" Effie asked, looking out the window into the empty blackness below.

"It has to," Zack said. "Unless . . ." He looked over at Omega Chimp, who was operating the ship's control panel. "Unless the planet has been destroyed!"

Zack stared at Omega Chimp in horror. "Get away from those controls, you foul, furry felon!" he cried.

"Zack, what's wrong with you?"

"What's wrong with *me*? You blasted that planet to subatomic scrap. It's the only explanation for why Bounceback hasn't returned. You murdered millions of innocent planet-dwelling planet-dwellers. And all those talented singing pigs besides! All because you didn't want to go to the opera. Why, you're no space hero at all. You're a music-hating space villain! A cosmic criminal, a monkey menace, a galactic goblin—"

Just then an alarm sounded and a blue light began flashing in the cockpit of the *Giant Slayer*.

"An emergency distress call!" Zack cried. "Don't they know we already have an emergency?"

Omega Chimp checked the computer console. "It's a class 3-C distress signal," he said. "A whole planet full of pigs is stuck in a wormhole."

"Whoever they are, they'll have to wait until I'm finished with you, you banana-loving ghoul! You destroyed Bounceback, and I must avenge them. Surrender, pajammied space menace! Your reign of terror is over!" Zack began a furious slap attack on Omega Chimp.

"Stop it!" Omega Chimp screamed.

SMACK!
WHACK!
SLAP!
SMACK!
SLAP!

"Give up, vile space meanie! I'll slap you silly. I'll smite you to smithereens. I'll—"

"Bounceback is sending the distress signal!" Omega Chimp screeched. "How many planets full of pigs sitting on the rim of wormholes do you think there are out there?"

"Just the two?" Zack asked.

"There's only one!"

SMACK!
WHACK!
SLAP!
SMACK!
WHACK!

CHAPTER TWELVE

No Parking Zone

Help us!" came the tailor's voice over the radio. "All these pigs have grown too fat. Now our planet is too heavy, and it's stuck in the wormhole."

"Well, that's easy to fix," Zack said. He snatched up the ship's microphone. "People of planet Bounceback, follow my instructions carefully. Starting today, put all the pigs on a diet. Cut down on sweets, give them ice water instead of soft drinks, and stop feeding them snacks at bedtime. Two months from now—three months, tops—your planet should pop right out."

Omega Chimp took the microphone away from Zack. "There's no sun in the wormhole. By this time tomorrow their entire planet will have frozen to death."

"Really?" asked the music teacher through the radio.

"Don't worry, people of Bounceback," Omega Chimp said, trying to calm the panicked planet. "I just sent out a distress call on the Astronet. Someone is sure to respond—"

SNATCH!

Bing! The computer signaled an incoming message.

"There, see? Help is already on the way." Omega Chimp looked at the message on his screen: *Glad to help. Can be there in three days.*

"Someone else is bound to reply," Zack said.

Bing!

Will be at your service in five days' time.

Bing!

How does a week from Saturday sound?

"Hello?" came the tailor's pitiful cry from the radio. "Are you still out there? Is somebody coming to help?"

"Oink?" added a frightened pig.

Zack, Omega Chimp, and Effie looked at one another.

"Hang in there, Bounceback," Omega Chimp said. "We're working on a plan right now."

"We are?" Effie asked.

"Sh!" said Omega Chimp, and covered the microphone. "I'm afraid it's hopeless. There's nothing we can do to save them."

"Help, it's dark in here and we're scared," the music teacher said. "Our pigs are scared too." A chorus of terrified pigs oinked in agreement.

"Can't we at least shine some light into the wormhole for them?" Zack asked.

"We'll need something really bright," Omega Chimp said. "I'll get the extra bulb for my landing lights from the storage closet." Omega Chimp headed for the back of the ship.

"Is that the big lightbulb that Commander Proton broke—?"* Effie began.

*As a matter of fact, it is! It happened in *The Adventures of Commander Zack Proton and the Warlords of Nibblecheese.*

Zack slapped a hand over Effie's speaker. "Sh!" Zack looked over his shoulder, but Omega Chimp was safely out of earshot. "He doesn't know about that. I got rid of the pieces in the trash ejector last week. We've got to find some other way of lighting up Bounceback." Zack spotted the dry-cleaning machine. "Hey, how about that ultraviolet light?" he said. "That's pretty bright."

"I can hook it up through the ship's scanner to direct the beam into the wormhole," Effie suggested.

"Let's do it!" they said together.

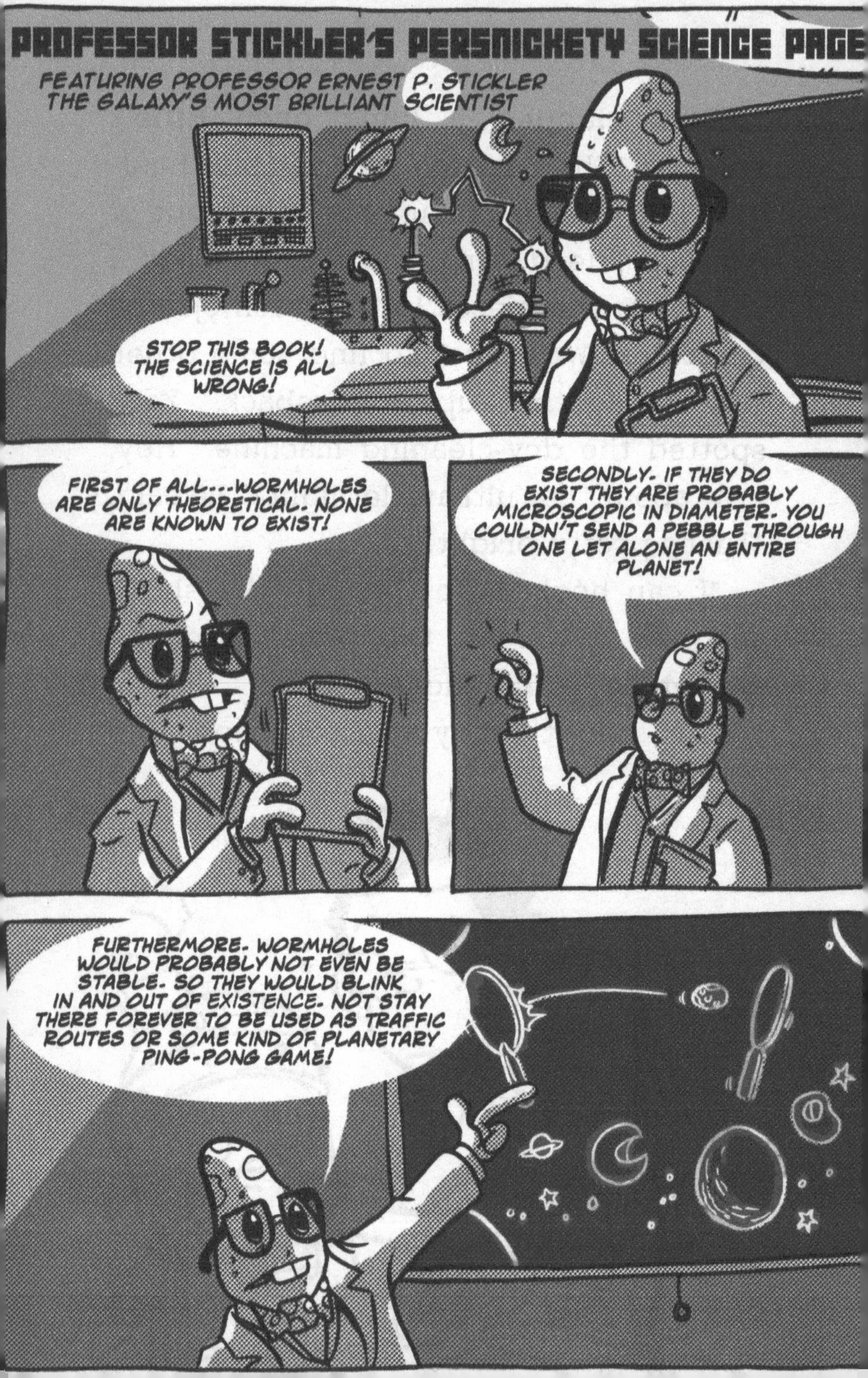
PROFESSOR STICKLER'S PERSNICKETY SCIENCE PAGE
FEATURING PROFESSOR ERNEST P. STICKLER
THE GALAXY'S MOST BRILLIANT SCIENTIST
STOP THIS BOOK! THE SCIENCE IS ALL WRONG!
FIRST OF ALL...WORMHOLES ARE ONLY THEORETICAL. NONE ARE KNOWN TO EXIST!
SECONDLY- IF THEY DO EXIST THEY ARE PROBABLY MICROSCOPIC IN DIAMETER. YOU COULDN'T SEND A PEBBLE THROUGH ONE LET ALONE AN ENTIRE PLANET!
FURTHERMORE. WORMHOLES WOULD PROBABLY NOT EVEN BE STABLE. SO THEY WOULD BLINK IN AND OUT OF EXISTENCE. NOT STAY THERE FOREVER TO BE USED AS TRAFFIC ROUTES OR SOME KIND OF PLANETARY PING-PONG GAME!

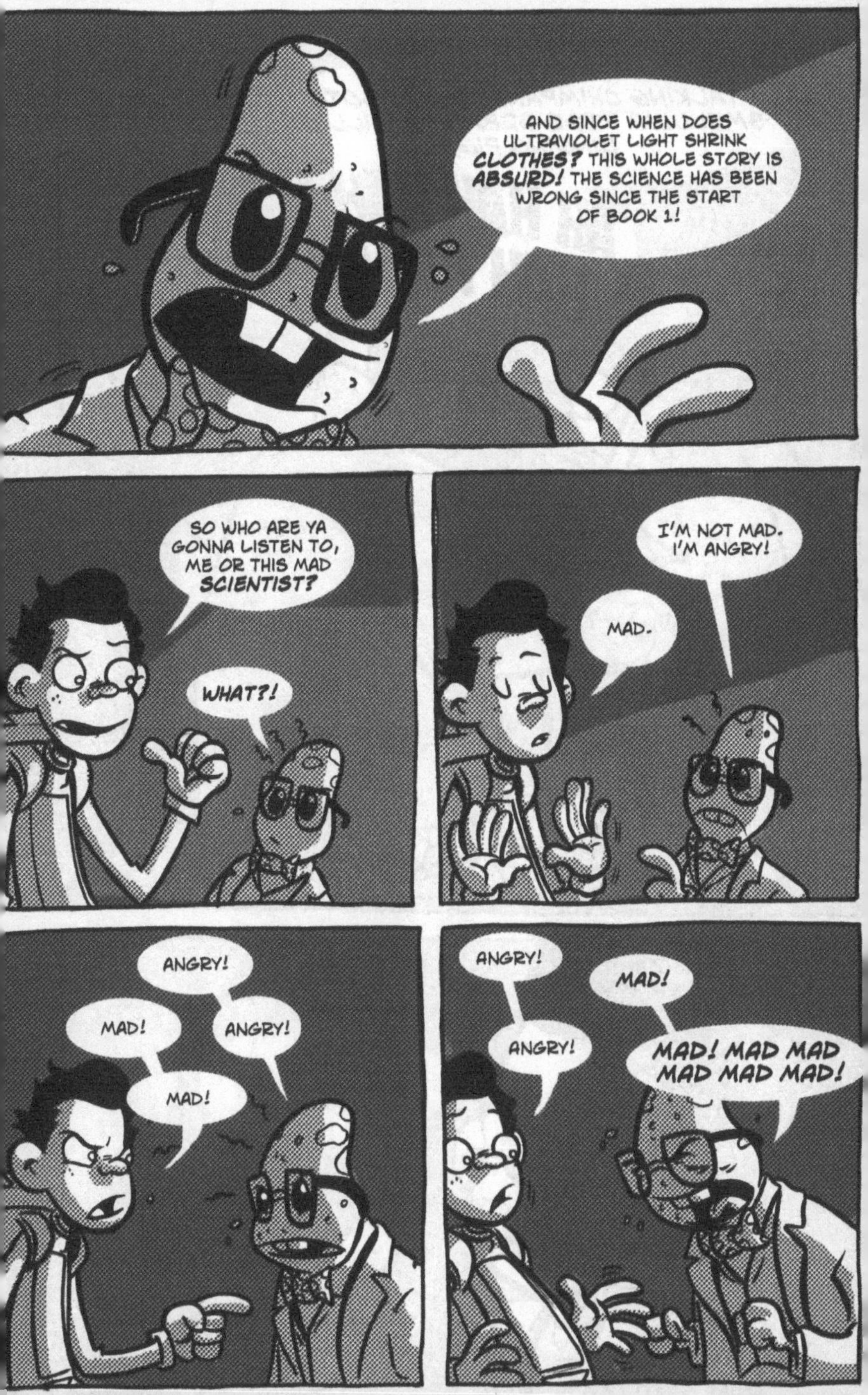
AND SINCE WHEN DOES ULTRAVIOLET LIGHT SHRINK CLOTHES? THIS WHOLE STORY IS ABSURD! THE SCIENCE HAS BEEN WRONG SINCE THE START OF BOOK 1!
SO WHO ARE YA GONNA LISTEN TO, ME OR THIS MAD SCIENTIST?
WHAT?!
I'M NOT MAD. I'M ANGRY!
MAD.
ANGRY!
MAD!
ANGRY!
MAD!
ANGRY!
MAD!
ANGRY!
MAD! MAD MAD MAD MAD MAD!

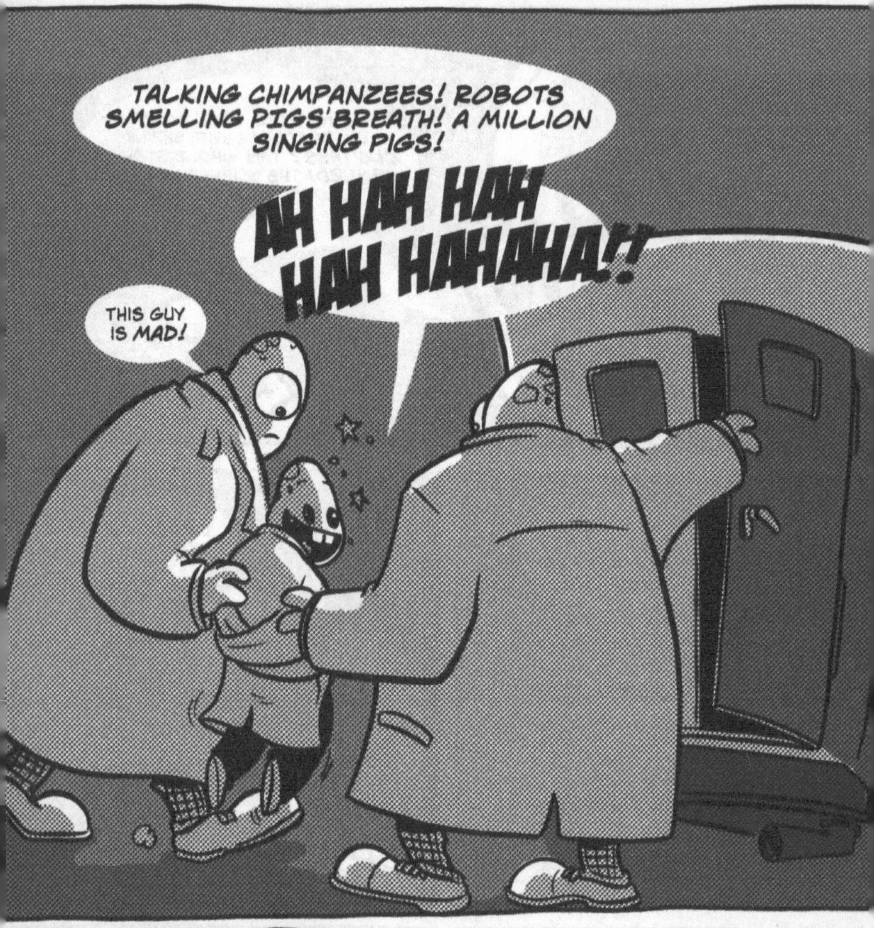
TALKING CHIMPANZEES! ROBOTS SMELLING PIGS' BREATH! A MILLION SINGING PIGS!
AH HAH HAH HAH HAHAHA!!
THIS GUY IS MAD!

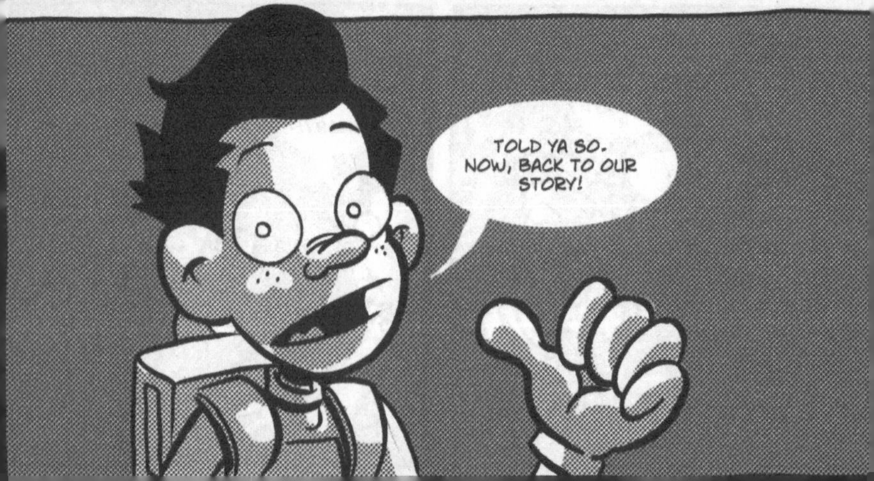
TOLD YA SO. NOW, BACK TO OUR STORY!

CHAPTER THIRTEEN

Let There Be Light

Omega Chimp searched the storage room for the third time. "I know that bulb is here somewhere," he said. Just then a terrible rattling noise came from the cockpit of the ship.

Omega Chimp raced to the front of the ship and found Zack and Effie standing over the ultraviolet cleaning machine with a tangle of wires running into the ship's computer console.

"What are you doing?" he screamed over the noise.

"We're being heroic!" Zack called back.

"It only *looks* foolish!" Effie added.

Then the whole ship started to shake. "Warning," said a voice from the control panel. "Stabilization system failure."

Omega Chimp punched some buttons on the control panel, and a diagram of his ship appeared. One section of the ship was outlined in red. "No wonder we're shaking like this," Omega Chimp said. "The high energy filters are missing from—"

"Warning!" the computer voice interrupted, and another section of the ship became outlined in red. Then another and another.

"Effie!" Omega Chimp screamed. "Half of the safety devices on this ship are missing! I told you not to use anything with a yellow safety tag on it!"

"I didn't," Effie said. "I took all the tags off first." He held up a wastebasket that was overflowing with yellow tags.

"Engines shutting down," said the computer voice. "Reducing life support. Primary power system overload. All systems failing." By now the entire diagram of the ship on the computer screen was outlined in red.

"That dry cleaner is sucking too much power," Omega Chimp said. "With all those safety devices gone—"

"Total ship destruction in ten seconds," warned the computer. "Ten . . . nine . . . eight . . . seven . . ."

"Turn it off!" Omega Chimp shouted at Zack.

"Good idea." Zack replied. "That countdown is really getting on my nerves."

"Not the computer, the dry cleaner! Unplug it!"

"Six . . . five . . . four . . ."

"I can't reach the plug!" Zack yelled.

"Three . . . two . . . one . . ."

Omega Chimp gritted his teeth, shut his eyes, and waited for "zero." But it never came. Instead the ship stopped shaking and the purple glow disappeared. All was quiet. Zack and Omega Chimp looked around and saw Effie with the plug in his hand at the end of a ten-foot-long mechanical arm.

"Did I do good?" Effie asked.

"Entering orbit over planet Bounce-back," said the computer voice, as though nothing had happened. They looked out the window and saw Bounceback right where it belonged. A huge cheer mixed with joyful oinking arose from the ship's radio.

"You did good, Effie," Zack said. "You're a genuine intergalactic space hero."

Effie's lights all shined brightly.

CHAPTER FOURTEEN

Some Pigs!

Zack, Omega Chimp, and Effie transported down to the planet to a hero's welcome. The first thing Omega Chimp noticed was the smell. The air on Bounceback was clean and fragrant.

"What happened to that horrible pig stench?" he asked. "And where are all the pigs?"

"Purple mini-pigs!" the tailor shouted. Omega Chimp looked down. One-inch-tall purple pigs frolicked happily around his ankles.

"And they smell daisy fresh!" added the music teacher.

"How did you do it?" the tailor asked.

"Well, we, um . . . ," Zack began. He looked at Omega Chimp. "How *did* we do it?" he asked.

"I must have left the ship's scanners set for pigs only," Omega Chimp said. "So when you hooked up the ultraviolet cleaner to the computer, it focused the light only on the pigs."

"And they shrunk all small and purply, just like your spacesuit," Zack said.

Omega Chimp glared at Effie. Effie whistled quietly and tried to look innocent.

The people of Bounceback were overjoyed to be free of the wormhole, and even more overjoyed to have tiny, fresh-smelling, purple pigs for pets.

"We're out of the opera business forever," the tailor said. The pigs oinked happily.

"These purple mini-pigs are the perfect pet," the music teacher added. "They're going to be an intergalactic sensation!" The people of Bounceback cheered, and swarms of tiny purple pigs bounced around their feet with joy.

"Just be careful where you step," Zack said.

The tailor called all his friends, and together they created a dozen new spacesuits in a rainbow of colors for Omega Chimp. The people of Bounceback also installed a real working dry-cleaning machine onboard Omega Chimp's ship. Meanwhile the music teacher gathered her best students to perform a free concert in honor of the three heroes.

There were many repairs to make to Omega Chimp's ship since Effie had taken pieces from just about every-where. A team of Bounceback engineers spent six hours fixing things and making adjustments on Omega Chimp's ship. They even gave the *Giant Slayer* a fresh coat of paint and a new name: *The Pig Shrinker*.

Soon it was time to go. The music teacher told Zack that the *Risky Rascal* had left Bounceback just an hour before Zack and Omega Chimp first arrived. "They took off in a pretty big hurry," she explained. "Something about getting the pig smell out of their ship before their captain finds out about it."

"Quick! Which way is the nearest shipwash station?" Zack asked.

"Thataway," an engineer said, pointing. "In the constellation Draco."

"Then off we go," Zack said, and jumped into the *Pig Shrinker*. Omega Chimp and Effie followed, and the door closed behind them.

"Wait!" the engineer cried. "When you get to Draco, look out for the—"

The engineer's words were drowned out by the *Pig Shrinker*'s engines as it took off into space.

"There goes a very foolish hero," the engineer said.

"Or a very heroic fool," the music teacher answered.

The tailor smiled. "Sometimes it can be very hard to tell the difference."

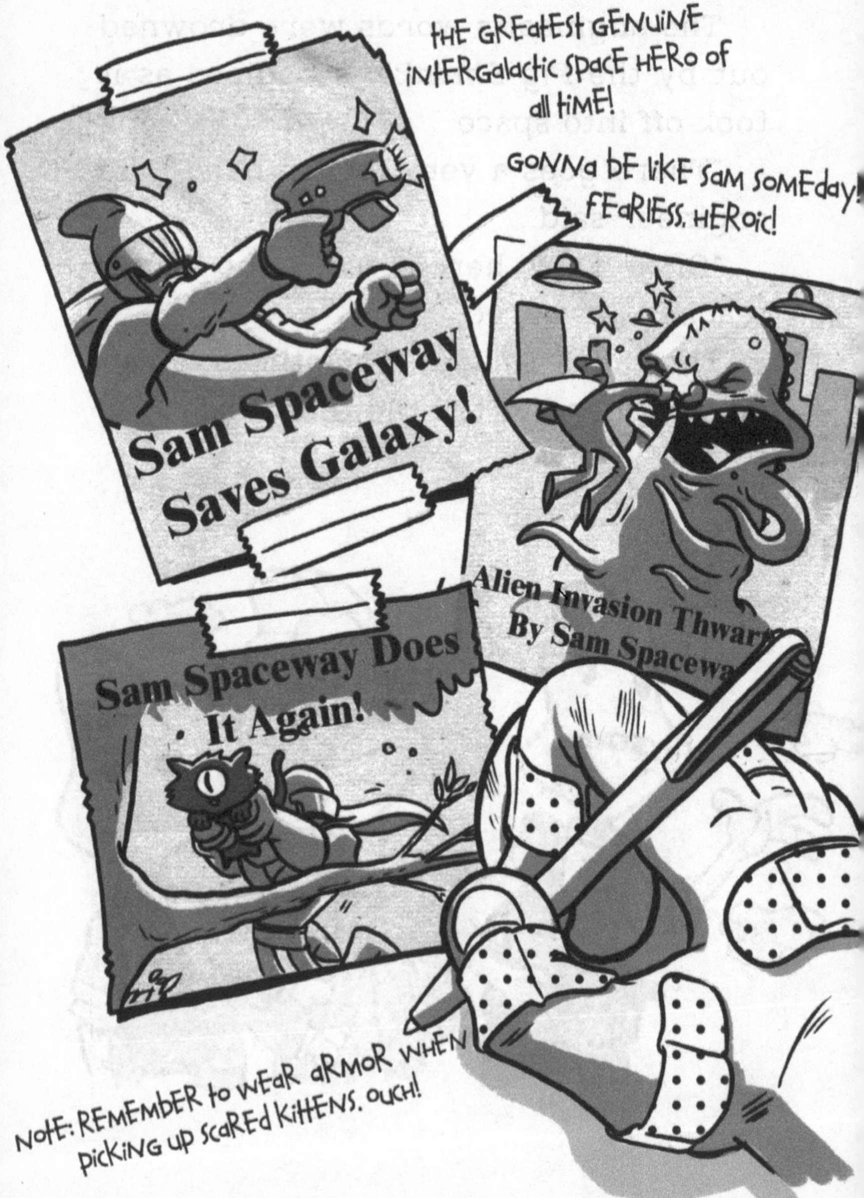
THE GREATEST GENUINE INTERGALACTIC SPACE HERO of all TIME!
GONNA BE LIKE SAM SOMEDAY! FEARLESS. HEROIC!
Sam Spaceway Saves Galaxy!
Alien Invasion Thwart
By Sam Spacewa
Sam Spaceway Does It Again!
NOTE: REMEMBER to WEAR ARMOR WHEN PICKING UP SCARED KITTENS. OUCH!